Samuel French Acting Edition

Theater Masters' Take Ten Volume VI

A Temporary Funeral for Darren McDuffy
by Brianna Barrett

The Game
by Lindsay Carpenter

How to Save the Polar Bear
by A.R. Corwin

Variable Rates of Kindness
by Cayenne Douglass

Break Through
by Erika Hakmiller

The Companion
by Matthew Libby

I0591868

Lady Bug Heaven
by Tony Mantia

ISBN 978-0-573-70908-1

www.concordtheatricals.com
www.concordtheatricals.co.uk

FOR PRODUCTION INQUIRIES

UNITED STATES AND CANADA
info@concordtheatricals.com
1-866-979-0447

UNITED KINGDOM AND EUROPE
licensing@concordtheatricals.co.uk
020-7054-7200

Each title is subject to availability from Concord Theatricals Corp., depending upon country of performance. Please be aware that *THEATER MASTERS' TAKE TEN VOLUME VI* may not be licensed by Concord Theatricals Corp. in your territory. Professional and amateur producers should contact the nearest Concord Theatricals Corp. office or licensing partner to verify availability.

Both amateurs and professionals considering a production are strongly advised to apply to the appropriate agent before starting rehearsals, advertising, or booking a theatre. A licensing fee must be paid whether the title(s) is presented for charity or gain and whether or not admission is charged. Professional/Stock licensing fees are quoted upon application to Concord Theatricals Corp.

This work is published by Samuel French, an imprint of Concord Theatricals Corp.

No one shall make any changes in this title(s) for the purpose of production. No part of this book may be reproduced, stored in a retrieval system, scanned, uploaded, or transmitted in any form, by any means, now known or yet to be invented, including mechanical, electronic, digital, photocopying, recording, videotaping, or otherwise, without the prior written permission of the publisher. No one shall share this title(s), or any part of this title(s), through any social media or file hosting websites.

For all inquiries regarding motion picture, television, online/digital and other media rights, please contact Concord Theatricals Corp.

MUSIC AND THIRD-PARTY MATERIALS USE NOTE

Licensees are solely responsible for obtaining formal written permission from copyright owners to use copyrighted music and/or other copyrighted third-party materials (e.g., artworks, logos) in the performance of this play and are strongly cautioned to do so. If no such permission is obtained by the licensee, then the licensee must use only original music and materials that the licensee owns and controls. Licensees are solely responsible and liable for clearances of all third-party copyrighted materials, including without limitation music, and shall indemnify the copyright owners of the play(s) and their licensing agent, Concord Theatricals Corp., against any costs, expenses, losses and liabilities arising from the use of such copyrighted third-party materials by licensees. For music, please contact the appropriate music licensing authority in your territory for the rights to any incidental music.

IMPORTANT BILLING AND CREDIT REQUIREMENTS

If you have obtained performance rights to this title, please refer to your licensing agreement for important billing and credit requirements.

THEATER MASTERS STAFF/BOARD

Daisy Walker, Executive Artistic Director
Victoria Hansen, Co-Artistic Director & Director of the Visionary Program
Kari Buckley, Artistic Administrator
Julia Hansen, Founder/Artistic Advisor

Advisory Board: Chris Ashley, Alec Baldwin, Andre Bishop, Scott Ellis, Doug Hughes, Judy Kaye, Andrew Leynse, John Lithgow, Robert Moss, Brian Murray, Jack O'Brien, Neil Pepe, Theresa Rebeck, John Rando, Tim Sanford, A.R. Gurney (emeritus, 1930-2017), Gordon Davidson (emeritus, 1933-2016)

Board of Directors: Leyla Bader, Susan Buckley, Danielle Chock, Nancy Dunlap, Julia Hansen, Victoria Hansen, Gerri Karetsky, Marianne Lubar, Amy Rose Marsh, Naomi McDougall Jones, Sofia Milonas, Virginia Pearce, Jessica Salet, Nancy Stevens, Charlotte Tripplehorn, Daisy Walker

THEATER MASTERS 2020 STAFF

Daisy Walker, Executive Artistic Director
Victoria Hansen, Co-Artistic Director & Director of the Visionary Program
Kari Buckley, Artistic Administrator
Julia Hansen, Founder/Artistic Advisor

TAKE TEN 2020 ZOOM READING TEAM

Julie Kramer, Director
Rachel Ackerman, Assistant Director

TAKE TEN 2020 NATIONAL ADVISORS

David Auburn & Craig Lucas

INTRODUCTION

Julia Hansen founded the National MFA Playwrights Competition and the Take Ten Festival in 2007 when she saw the need to bridge the gap between the academic training playwrights were receiving and the professional careers that lay ahead of them.

Take Ten's professional development opportunities and partnership with Concord Theatricals provide playwrights with a career-igniting entrance into the entertainment industry and introduce their work to the American theatre.

Each year, we invite MFA playwrights from some of the top dramatic writing programs in the country to submit a ten-minute play. In the spring, the six-to-ten winning playwrights are flown to New York for an Equity showcase production of their plays featuring professional directors and actors. When Covid-19 hit in March 2020, we quickly had to figure out a way to give these talented students a meaningful and substantial experience within virtual perimeters. We wanted to fulfill our promse of Take Ten – to launch these young playwrights into the industry and provide a platform from which to share their unique voices in American theatre.

We rose to the challenge: we produced Zoom readings of each of their plays with the promised professional artists. We arranged meetings with industry professionals from around the country. These seven playwrights were mentored by Craig Lucas and David Auburn, who gave feedback and helped guide them through rewrites. And the best prize of all – their plays are living on past this pandemic by being published by Concord Theatricals.

We are grateful to all who have supported our 2020 National MFA Playwrights Festival: the MFA programs across the country, including Arizona State University, Brown University, Carnegie Mellon University, Northwestern University, NYU, University of Iowa, University of Texas at Austin, UCLA, UCSD, and the Yale School of Drama, who recognize talented students; our director Julie Kramer, who shared her time, expertise, and vision with our artists; our actors from far and wide who lent their talents; and finally, our generous individual donors and Board of Directors who make Take Ten possible.

We are passionate about these playwrights, and we hope you will enjoy this sixth anthology of Theater Masters' plays.

Sincerely,
Daisy Walker, *Executive Artistic Director*
Vicky Hansen, *Co-Artistic Director &*
Director of the Visionary Program

TABLE OF CONTENTS

A Temporary Funeral for Darren McDuffy

Brianna Barrett

A TEMPORARY FUNERAL FOR DARREN MCDUFFY received a virtual reading on May 14, 2020, produced by Theater Masters and directed by Julie Kramer. The cast was as follows:

HOST	Willie Mosley
NANA	Wendy Perkins
JANTIS	Morgan Walsh
GENERAL	Kirk McGee
LORELEI	Allegra Epstein

A TEMPORARY FUNERAL FOR DARREN MCDUFFY was produced by Naked Angels on December 3, 2019 at Thymele Arts. The director was Allison Youngberg, and the cast was as follows:

HOST	Christopher T. Wood
NANA	Torie Tyson
JANTIS	Lorn Conner
GENERAL	James Kulick
LORELEI	Ashley Spillers

CHARACTERS

HOST – male, fifty-plus
NANA – female, sixty-plus
JANTIS – male, fifty-plus
GENERAL – male, late thirties but haggard
LORE – female, twenty to thirty

SETTING

A funeral taking place wherever you are.
Consider the audience may be funeral guests,
with our cast of characters sitting among them.

TIME

It doesn't exist anymore. And it's all we have.

AUTHOR'S NOTES

Considerations

Are you performing this piece as part of a festival of multiple ten-minute plays? Well! To make the congregation sound large when everyone speaks in unison, consider asking actors from the other plays to help out with this one line. It's at the very beginning! The more immersive it sounds, the better. And seriously, who doesn't hate that guy who cut them off in traffic?

Dedicated to my friend, John Maggi

(A choral song plays as the lights come up.
A **MAN** in all black [a priest?] stands at a
podium before a group of **MOURNERS**.)*

HOST. We are gathered here today to say goodbye to Darren
McDuffy. We regret that we only got to know him for
a short time. As hard as it is for some of us to accept,
we know he's gone to a better place. And we know, no
matter how long it takes, we will see him again.

In good time.

Until then, he will be reunited with

his wife, Cathy.

His children.

His parents.

His boss.

His dealer.

His neighbor Steve he doesn't really like that much.

The mailman.

The people at the market.

And all the bastards in traffic – including the guy in the
red Chevy Silverado that flipped him off last week after
blocking him from changing lanes in time to catch his
exit.

---

*A license to produce *A Temporary Funeral for Darren McDuffy* does
not include a performance license for any third-party or copyrighted
music. Licensees should create an original composition or use music in
the public domain. For further information, please see Music and Third-
Party Materials Use Note on page iii.

JANTIS. Fuck that guy!

> *(A hush falls. Everyone takes a deep breath. Then, the entire congregation breathes the same phrase, peacefully, in unison:)*

ALL. Fuck that guy.

HOST. Truly, life is wasted on the living.

But as you know, Darren didn't die in traffic. That'd be too...well, *pedestrian*. If you'll pardon the pun...

Quick show of hands: How many people *knew* Darren?

Ah, okay, just a few of you.

For those of you who did, or even those who didn't, I do want to make space for anyone to get up and say anything as they are so moved.

Knowing him or what he would have wanted is *not* a requirement, as long as you have something to say – preferably something that sounds deep or makes you feel better about your own

lonely...

empty...

pitiful set of circumstances.

But first, I'd like to invite Edith "Nana" McDuffy to share a few words. Edith is Darren's paternal grandmother. She died in 2012.

Edith?

NANA. Hello, my goodness, I didn't expect to be here. So sudden!

Darren was a nice boy. He'd come to visit in the summers with his parents – nothing fancy, mind you... I wasn't a tea and crumpets kind of grandma. All I had was a little trailer in Las Vegas, but he'd get so excited to come see me. Boy after my own heart...it's a shame, too. Same heart, same heart condition, right?

LORE. But he didn't die of a heart condition...

NANA. Who are you, the medical examiner?

As I was saying about Darren: He's a nice young man. When his heart stopped for those glorious forty-six seconds – you can imagine how excited I was!

A gran-kid! Finally! None of my own kids have had the good sense to die.

Last I saw Darren was Christmas at the nursing home... My hearing had gotten so bad I barely knew *what* was going on, and they didn't really try...just talked around me and over me for an hour or so, until they'd get bored and leave.

JANTIS. Life is as cruel and as selfish as the living.

NANA. Darren used to write me letters, as a boy. Before he got into *social mediums*.

You save a lot on postage shouting into the void.

After I died, years ago, he put a picture of me up on his Faceygram or whatever it is. An old portrait of me from when I was thirty-nine, from that day Henry made us go get family portraits at the church.

(She pulls out a crumpled copy of the photo to show everyone.)

That's a thing people do – share young photos of their dead elders. The living seem to like that reminder that their old-fogey relatives used to be healthy and spry. A meditation on mortality, I s'pect. Or proof that they had good genes even though we all end up fat.

JANTIS. Hey, I'm in the best shape of my life.

NANA. You're *dead*.

JANTIS. Lowered my cholesterol!

> *(This should be the first time the audience gets a good look at **JANTIS**, and he is very obviously deceased. Maybe an axe is lodged in his chest? Life is short – get creative!)*

NANA. Jantis here makes me grateful I died in my sleep.

JANTIS. I don't love wearing my murder weapon around, but I'm a lot better off than the guys who died in the shower.

NANA. AS I WAS SAYING. When my grandson Darren's heart stopped, I was first in line to see him. Not a lot of competition what with most his friends and family still living. We'd grown apart while we were both still alive, but death has a way of bringing people together. I was ready to be his primary dead friend!

I said, "Hello."

And he was so stunned he said nothing.

I reached out to touch him and –

poof!

He was sucked right back to Earth.

Paramedics got to him.

HOST. It's always the good ones who are taken from us too soon.

NANA. Now he's talking about what a "life-changing" experience it was to see me. He's gonna turn his whole life around! Get sober, clean living, exercise, the whole thing.

HOST. Do you think he believes in...the place upstairs?

NANA. I think he thought this *was* the place upstairs! Poor fool. He's goin' on about bright lights and what not – says I told him, *"Noooow is not your tiiime."*

– But I didn't say that shit! I said, "*Hooow un-sat-is-fyyyyyn.*"

Cuz I saw he was leavin'! I get sick of hangin' out with all you cottonheads all eternity!

No offense.

And of course we're pleased to have little Jimmy and Eva here with us – the day your mom drowned you both in a bathtub was the happiest day of my purgatory.

> *(She smiles warmly.)*

Kids don't often end up here but they were little monsters. Anyway, I've yammered on for long enough. I know a lot of you didn't get to meet Darren, since he was with us such a short while. I only hope he gets over this spiritual kick, falls off the wagon and gets back here sooner rather than later. Thank you.

HOST. Thank you for that, Edith. I know Darren has many family members in attendance today, from his grandparents to great-grandparents to great-great-grandparents and so on. I'll open the floor to anyone else who'd like to say a few words.

> *(A Civil War **GENERAL** drunkenly hobbles toward the podium. He has visible war wounds.)*

GENERAL. Well how-*doo*! I'm General Walter Akers Frey of the Thirty-first Battalion. Of course I never met the young man in question but I'm tempted to say good riddance to 'im. Not intending to be crass here, with all respect to the dead...

> *(He gestures to include the group of dead guests before him.)*

...I reckon we could do better.

Now I say this as a man who fought and died in a war – a dumb war that I was on the wrong side of, frankly, but at least I was fighting for something. This young man – a distant cousin of mine – what's he go and do? Get bored and off himself on accident? My utter apologies but it sounds to me like they're just making life too easy nowadays.

LORE. Oookay, General, let's take a seat now –

GENERAL. And yes I've had a few whiskeys! What else is there to do?

LORE. *(Walking him back to his seat.)* You look familiar – I must recognize you from one of the Ken Burns documentaries my dad always has on.

GENERAL. Yeah yeah, I wanted to sit down. I've earned sitting down. I stood up for something.

HOST. *(To* **LORE.***)* Thank you, young lady, please come up here and share a few words.

LORE. Me? No I'm not going to mourn that he isn't dead anymore.

You know what happened, right? Why he died?

Why he didn't?

Isn't he in a better place?

HOST. Funerals are for the funeral-er, not the funeral-ee. The fact is he was here and now he's gone. I mean! How many of us have had to listen to the haphazard guessing of mortals – "This is what he would have wanted," and, "If she were here right now, she'd say..." Nobody says that for the benefit of the dead.

LORE. Yeah...

I always wanted to be donated to science. But I'm not!

No one will ever look at me closely...

NANA. I was embalmed, and trust me, it was no picnic. Plugs straight up everything!

HOST. My point is simply that we needn't dwell on where Darren is now – better or worse, and it is certainly better. But *we* are worse off and *that* is what this is about.

Can you introduce yourself and how you know the recently un-deceased?

LORE. Oh. I'm Lorelei... He called me "Lore."

We used to date back in college. And...

C'mon, we all wish our exes were dead, right?

HOST. You and me both, sister.

LORE. Ah, k, that feels weird I'mgonnago...

NANA. Now you wait a dagnab minute there. You knew my Darren? Really knew him?

LORE. ...I died like him but I didn't come back.

I don't remember what I was thinking. If I was trying to live too much or not at all...

I woulda asked him. It would have been nice to see him again.

(*A beat.*)

He had a morbid sense of humor. Used to say he wanted the kind of headstone that would make someone *wonder* about him.

Like, "Darren McDuffy – he died as he lived. But with fewer bees."

Or, "Darren McDuffy, now he can't talk about what happened in Vegas."

JANTIS. "Here lies Darren McDuffy – after all that, he finally found a parking spot."

LORE. You got it. That's the joke.

He'd always come and watch my band play. He was also a drug addict with crippling anxiety and enough self-loathing that you could power a small city if you found some way to bottle it, but. He'd come alive when you'd least expect it – when you needed it, he'd start singing your favorite song and you didn't even know he knew the words. He used to say, "Promise we'll never grow old." And I did.

...And

I didn't.

NANA. It's not all it's cracked up to be. Another sixty years, what's the difference if you end up here anyway? Now he has hope. False hope, it seems to me! Do you want that for Darren? When he was *this close* to knowing there's no reason to try cuz there's *nothing here*?

LORE. But now he's back where the *Something* is. He can go outside, smell the air...bonfires, cigarettes and sand castles...his kids blowing bubbles and making chalk outlines of their bodies just for fun...he has everything there is.

NANA. Yeah: Global warming, aging, ugly sweaters, paying the bills, social meteors –

JANTIS. – *Actual* meteors. And fake news, and regular news...

GENERAL. War, political divides, corruption.

LORE. Sure, fine, life is an endurance test that doesn't end 'til you lose. "Mattering" is a lie we tell ourselves to keep going until we can't anymore. But I felt it for a minute. Even as I was playing music in crappy bars with nobody there who wasn't shouting over the sound of the songs I wrote for my guitarist who never showered and never ate and had a coke problem and just wanted *someone* to look at her closely and –

...Yeah, I *was* the guitarist in my band...

NANA. Did you know *music* is the one way we can communicate from the beyond?

LORE. ...The day I killed myself, I thought of him.

I thought, "Darren would really get this."

"...I guess I should have stayed in touch..."

NANA. So sing to him, play the siren, call him back! Crush him with your memory or he'll forget you by the time he dies! And then what will you have? No need to be a good person now, we're stuck here – we'll *never* get upstairs. Isn't that right, Pastor?

HOST. Oh – who knows. I mean, *I'm* here, and I did *not* do anything *weird* while I was alive. Are we all clear on that?

JANTIS. Oh, I did weird stuff.

GENERAL. Ha! By modern standards I don't know that *anything* I did can be justified!

NANA. Look, we don't know if there's a heaven, but we know this ain't it.

Now he's out trying to learn life is worth living

and maybe it's not.

Look around you.

Why give him a false sense of hope?

(**LORE** *looks around at the nothingness.*)

LORE. Because time is all he has.

...Time is all we have...

(A choral song plays.)*

(LORE *lights a candle and hums along with the song. Soon, all we can see is candlelight.)*

End of Play

---

*A license to produce *A Temporary Funeral for Darren McDuffy* does not include a performance license for any third-party or copyrighted music. Licensees should create an original composition or use music in the public domain. For further information, please see Music and Third-Party Materials Use Note on page iii.

The Game

Lindsay Carpenter

THE GAME was first workshopped at New York University Tisch's "Bespoke Festival" in New York, New York on March 27, 2019. The cast was as follows:

HER . . . . Sydney Elisabeth
HIM . . . . Joey Shaw

THE GAME was first produced by Broke People Play Festival in New York, New York on November 9, 2019. It was directed by Olivia Kormos. The cast was as follows:

HER . . . . .Alexia Marza
HIM . . . . .Jack Delaney

THE GAME received a virtual reading on May 16, 2020, produced by Theater Masters and directed by Julie Kramer. The cast was as follows:

HER . . . . .Spring Snyder
HIM . . . . .David Fraioli

CHARACTERS

HER – Focused, impatient, brave. Does not like to be vulnerable.

HIM – Shy, curious, awestruck. Increasingly comfortable in his own skin.

A Note on Casting

Contrary to the pronouns used, "Her" can be played by an actor of any gender. For the purposes of the anachronistic time period, "Him" should be played by someone who identifies as male. If the gender of "Her" is switched, the name in the program should also switch (to "Him" or "They." It's okay if there are two "Hims.")

SETTING

Mid-14th-Century Europe. Sort of.

AUTHOR'S NOTES

The transition between each section should be marked or cued by the snap of the character Her's fingers. Transitions should be fast and fluid.

Embrace the magical realism, don't try to render anything too realistically. The aging of the characters should be subtle hints at their ages, rather than caricatures.

You can change the feather colors (gray and yellow) to match those you find, preferably colors other than black and white.

A slash (/) indicates an overlap in dialogue. The next line should begin when the slash occurs.

FIRST GAME: FAIRY KINGDOM

> *(HER is twelve. She sits, playing in the dirt, building a fairy kingdom. HIM, also twelve, appears from the other side of the stage. He watches HER.)*

HER. *(Not looking up.)* Toad or newt?

HIM. S-s-sorry?

HER. I could make you a cat, if that's your preference.

HIM. No!

> *(She waves HER arm. He flinches. She laughs.)*

> *(He gives HER something wrapped in cloth.)*

HER. What is it?

HIM. My uncle's real nice, I swear. He always gives me two spoonfuls more than everyone when my ma's not looking. If you just give him a chance –

HER. Who's your uncle?

HIM. Merek.

HER. I didn't curse him.

HIM. He's really sick.

HER. I didn't curse him.

HIM. Oh. I'm sorry. I guess I – are you sure?

> *(Off her glare.)* Can you make him better?

HER. *(Sighs.)* Hide some rosemary under his pillow. And, uh...kiss him on the forehead as soon as he wakes up.

HIM. That'll make him better?

HER. *(She considers lying.)* No. But the rosemary will smell nice while he's asleep and kisses first thing in the morning will make him happy while he dies.

HIM. Can't you fix him? I could –

HER. No.

> *(He looks like he may cry. She continues playing in the dirt. He doesn't leave.)*

> *(Finally she glares at* **HIM** *expectantly. He doesn't leave.)*

Sit. It's a fairy kingdom. Take the stick. Dig.

HIM. Is it magic?

HER. Only if you think it is.

HIM. Then why do you do it?

HER. It's a game.

> *(She SNAPS her fingers.)*

SECOND GAME: GUESSES

*(A shift. They are seventeen. They are back to
back now. He is annoyed, but she can't see.)*

HER. Um, tall.

HIM. Like, taller than me or –?

HER. Way taller than you.

HIM. Okay, so a giant.

HER. He's not a giant. He, um...oh, he just started to play
the lute.

HIM. So, not a peasant.

HER. No, he lives in the castle. But, he's not, you know, one
of them.

HIM. How do you know him?

HER. You have to guess first. That'll give it away.

HIM. I don't know anyone in the castle. Especially not a
big, stupid lute player.

HER. You know him. Guess.

HIM. Crewe.

HER. You know it's not Crewe.

(He gets up, leaving.)

Keep guessing. Come on. Where are you going?

HIM. This is stupid.

HER. Okay, you go. Describe who you like.

HIM. We're not kids anymore.

HER. It's fun. It's not like they'll ever notice us...well, you
maybe but. I'm the... I'm the kid who played with fairy
kingdoms and / can brew you a fix for a shilling.

HIM. With me. You played fairy kingdoms with me.

HER. They don't see you that way.

HIM. I am that way.

HER. You're still respectable, normal, they don't think you're a witch –

HIM. Okay, you want to guess? I'll describe her, I'll describe who I like.

(Looking right at **HER.***)* She memorizes little bits of speeches 'cause she thinks it's fun, her bed is covered in flowers she swears she never planted, / soft skin, terrifying eyes, and / the most...

HER. *(At first slash.)* Don't.

(At second slash.) Don't.

HIM. Don't you want to guess?

HER. I don't.

HIM. You don't. Because of the giant lute player –

HER. Because *I don't.*

(She SNAPS.)

THIRD GAME: CONTACT

(Mid-twenties now. They make out. Frantically. Finally they part, tired from the long bout.)

HER. When's she back?

HIM. She went to the alewife. They'll talk for hours.

HER. When'd she leave?

HIM. Seconds before you got here. I made a wish for you, I put rosemary at the window so you'd –

HER. Rosemary doesn't do anything. Now if you really want to make me fall in love with you, I heard you can combine mandrake root and...

(Points to her crotch.)

...blood and –

HIM. That's – no.

HER. Or, you can bake a cake and rub it over every orifice buck naked –

HIM. Please.

HER. *I'd* watch that. Anyways, it's supposed to be a very effective love potion.

HIM. I don't think I need a love potion for you anymore.

HER. No?

HIM. No...

(She breaks away. He's right.)

HER. What, do you think I'm in love with you? That we'll become husband and wife because I like to...suck... parts of you now and again?

(Mocking.) Wittle wifey is scared 'cause you were gone all day? Do you love me, wittle husband? Do you want

to have a hundwed babies until we can't hear each other in our tewibwy woud house and we can't find each other between all the tewible childwen –?

> *(He steps to her, and she shuts up. He kisses her. Not passionately, just clearly.)*

HIM. I don't want to *play* husband and wife with you.

HER. *(Weak, not sure she believes it.)* I don't...

HIM. Still?

HER. *(Certain.) I don't.*

> *(She SNAPS.)*

FOURTH GAME: DEATH

(Age thirty now. They stand side by side, hand in hand. He is devastated. They stare down at something [his wife's dead body].)

HIM. I miss her screaming.

HER. We should burn her.

HIM. I can't.

HER. We need to burn her body. That's what the church says we have to do.

HIM. She's my wife.

HER. She's dead.

(He removes his hand from hers.)

HIM. I thought I could save her. I thought if I prayed and if I prayed... Then the fever. That if I did it right, if I... chopped up a snake, force-fed her vinegar, whipped myself in case it was *my* sin – us – burst her when she swelled, wiped away the pus. Then headaches, chills. And the screaming. As long as she was screaming she was still alive.

HER. Everyone is dying. There's nothing we can do.

HIM. Built a fire next to her to drive out the fever, rubbed onions on her body, bled her, fed her horseradish until she cried, leeches –

HER. It's terrible and it's ugly, but there's nothing –

HIM. Do you care? Do you care she's dead? Did you curse her? Did you wish for her –? She hated you. She didn't care about *us*, didn't care that I woke up next to someone else. But *you*. She hated you. Anyone but you. And I just, I let her think I didn't care. I made her think you were the world to me. Did she give up? Did she just give up on me and die?

HER. I don't think sex with me caused the plague.

HIM. I'm tired.

HER. We'll rest. We just have to burn the body.

HIM. Thea.

HER. Okay. Thea. We just have to burn Thea... It's going to be us soon. It has to be us soon. Why would *we* get to live.

And. And before that happens, I want you with me.

I do.

(*Worst timing ever. He turns to stone.*)

HIM. I have to burn my wife.

(*She SNAPS.*)

FIFTH GAME: FEATHERS

(They're old now. He's seated again, playing in the dirt with a stick. She walks in, realizes he's there.)

(They haven't spoken since the end of the fourth scene. In that time, two-thirds of everyone they know has died. This time, she's the one who's tentative.)

HER. Sorry.

(Notices what he's doing.)

A fairy kingdom?

HIM. Our first game... You look like one now. A witch. The wrinkles and the black clothes, the... I hear you run the alehouse now. Brew beer, seduce defenseless men, deflower virgins, and own cats.

HER. The cat part is true.

HIM. You always liked cats.

HER. I almost turned you into one. Once.

HIM. Right. Might have been the better move... I'd like to be a hawk. I guess.

(She says nothing.)

It seems like a small enough favor after everything.

HER. What would you do? As a hawk?

HIM. The feathers. Height. And the wind. I could see anything. Go anywhere. Plus I could shit on the heads of people I didn't like.

HER. Okay.

HIM. You'll do it?

HER. Do you really want me to?

> *(He didn't think she could. Now he's not so sure.)*

HIM. Is it a game?

HER. Only if you think it is.

HIM. What does it take?

HER. *(Doing it as she speaks.)* I put feathers in a jar. Gray and yellow. Many feathers. And you draw.

HIM. And if it's gray?

> *(She SNAPS her fingers. They step to the right and he becomes a hawk. Maybe he turns his back to the audience and crouches. He tests out a wing.)*

> *(She SNAPS again. They step back to where they were and resume.)*

HER. You become a hawk. You fly away, free, and I've proved I'm a witch.

HIM. And if it's yellow?

> *(She SNAPS again. This time they step left. Their hands touch. They intermingle. They kiss.)*

> *(She SNAPS again. They step back.)*

HER. I guess I'm not a witch. And you're still a man. And maybe we...maybe there's a chance for us. Okay?

> *(He nods, uncertain. She shuffles the feathers. The audience can see them, swirling in the jar. He starts to reach into the jar.)*

Close your eyes.

I can't come with you. If you change. I can't become a bird.

HIM. Is this a game?

> *(She offers him the jar. Vulnerable. He closes his eyes and reaches in so the audience can see. He pulls out a feather and holds it up.)*

[If it's a gray feather:]

> *(He becomes a hawk. Maybe he turn his back to the audience and crouches.)*

HER. *(Trying not to break down.)* Okay. Okay. Hey little one. Hey. It's okay. Just test them out.

> *(He tests out one wing. Then the other.)*

Do they feel all right? You're the first bird I've made. Can I touch you?

> *(He takes a step closer to her. She touches him.)*

They're so soft. ... Do you have to leave? Do you have to leave me now? ... You could pick again. Maybe you could pick again. Maybe you could pick me.

End of Play

[If it's a yellow feather:]

HER. I guess I'm not a witch. I guess it was just another game. I wanted it to work. For you. ... I just – I don't want to stop having games with you.

> *(A tense beat. Then:)*

HIM. "Sit. Take the stick. Dig."

HER. *(Sitting, smiling, remembering.)* "Is it magic?"

HIM. "Only if you think it is."

HER. "Then why do you do it?"

> *(As they dig, their hands touch. They intermingle. He smiles.)*

HIM. "It's a game."

> *(They kiss.)*

End of Play

How to Save the Polar Bear

A.R. Corwin

HOW TO SAVE THE POLAR BEAR received its first virtual reading on May 14, 2020, produced by Theater Masters and directed by Julie Kramer. The cast was as follows:

POLE	Elisha Lawson
JOURNALIST	Eileen Seeley
CAMERAPERSON	Kari Buckley

This play was a 2020 Regional Finalist for the Kennedy Center American College Theater Festival Gary Garrison National Ten-Minute Play Award.

CHARACTERS

POLE – an emaciated polar bear
JOURNALIST – a human
CAMERAPERSON – a human

SETTING

A desolate spot somewhere in the Arctic Circle.

TIME

The present, or possibly the past –
depending on when you read this play.

AUTHOR'S NOTES

All characters may be played by actors of any ethnicity, gender, and age. However, the way the play is cast may bring out additional subtext. I ask that directors pay special attention to this.

Pole's pronoun should remain as "it," no matter the gender of the actor who plays Pole.

(Lights up on **POLE** *sitting upright but asleep, supported by a jagged block of ice. It is surrounded by piles of trash: old newspapers, food wrappers, take-out containers, etc. Beside it is a worn-out cardboard sign with the words "Picture with a Polar Bear – $50 NO FREEBIES!!")*

(The **JOURNALIST** *and* **CAMERAPERSON**, *both wearing winter jackets and boots, enter. The* **CAMERAPERSON** *carries a large camera bag. They both stop when they see* **POLE**. *Excitement.)*

JOURNALIST. *(Quietly.)* Finally!

(Takes out audio recorder.)

Arctic Circle, day four. First polar bear sighting.

CAMERAPERSON. *(Takes out camera.)* ...What's that smell?

(They both sniff the air and realize it's **POLE**.*)*

...Maybe we should look for a different one.

JOURNALIST. No, this one's perfect. Grungy, emaciated – super compelling.

CAMERAPERSON. I don't know...

JOURNALIST. We can always Photoshop it.

(The **CAMERAPERSON** *takes a few test shots. There is a click noise with each photo.)*

Get one of me looking at it. Like this.

(The **JOURNALIST** *looks concernedly at* **POLE.** *The* **CAMERAPERSON** *takes a photo and looks at the screen.)*

CAMERAPERSON. Looks great. This could be the cover shot.

(Begins putting away camera.)

Let's go.

JOURNALIST. Are you kidding me? *We gotta talk to it!* Get out the video camera.

(The **JOURNALIST** *takes the camera as the* **CAMERAPERSON** *takes out a video camera.)*

(Walks up close to **POLE.***)* Start recording.

CAMERAPERSON. What are you doing? Don't get so close –

JOURNALIST. It's time to poke the bear.

CAMERAPERSON. No, wait –

(The **JOURNALIST** *takes a photo right in* **POLE***'s face, which emits a flash and a click noise.* **POLE** *wakes up with a start. The* **JOURNALIST** *quickly steps back.)*

POLE. Huh? Wha–? Hey – Hey! What do you think you're doing?

JOURNALIST. Good afternoon. Sorry to wake you –

POLE. Hey, can't you people read? That's fifty dollars!

(Notices the video camera.)

Hey! Video's *extra*!

JOURNALIST. Okay, okay, we'll stop.

(As **POLE** *stands up, the* **JOURNALIST** *surreptitiously signals for the* **CAMERAPERSON** *to keep filming.)*

We were just so excited to see you. We're journalists from –

POLE. I don't care who you are – you took a photo, I want my money.

JOURNALIST. Journalists can't pay for photos. We have to follow certain ethical standards –

POLE. *(Getting in their faces.)* Did you ask my permission to take that photo? No. So your "ethical standards" can go kiss my furry, white butt!

CAMERAPERSON. *(Scared.)* Come on, let's go –

JOURNALIST. Relax. I got this. *Just keep recording.*

(To **POLE.***)* We just want to know what it's like, with all the changes up here. How you're *surviving.*

POLE. *Surviving.* Yeah, sure. I'm surviving all right.

JOURNALIST. We'd love to interview you –

POLE. Not interested.

JOURNALIST. Wait, just hear me out –

POLE. I don't need to. I already know what you want. You're looking for a sob story, right?

JOURNALIST. *(Laughs.)* Uh –

POLE. "Boo hoo, the poor polar bear. Look at how sad it is. It's losing its home. But look at me, look at how much *I care.* Because *I'm* a good person." And then you pack up and run off to win your Pulitzers and shit.

JOURNALIST. A bear who knows about the Pulitzer!

POLE. Damn right I know about the Pulitzer! A photo of my bony ass could win twenty of 'em! I got journalists up here all the time, leaning outta helicopters, takin' photos of me while I'm sleeping, while I'm taking a dump – I don't got any goddamn privacy! And I don't see a dime for any of it. Well I'm not having it – a-ny-more!

JOURNALIST. I think we got off on the wrong foot. We aren't here to bother you. We want to help you. Imagine, on the very front page, "The Story Behind the Starving Polar Bear." You'll get millions of fans all over the world.

POLE. Millions of fans? Yeah, right.

JOURNALIST. No, really! We've done it before! Right?

CAMERAPERSON. Yeah, have you seen that video of the sea turtle? The one with the straw up its nose?

POLE. Yeah, I saw that, poor bastard. Looked painful.

CAMERAPERSON. That was us. I shot that.

JOURNALIST. Yeah, and I interviewed it. And now it has like, five hundred thousand followers, right? Five hundred thousand people who *care* about it. Who want to help it. And we want to do the same thing for you... What do you say?

POLE. ...All right, I'll do it.

JOURNALIST. Great!

POLE. – If you give me ten K.

CAMERAPERSON. ...Excuse me?

POLE. You heard me.

JOURNALIST. *Bear* – ...I-I'm sorry, I haven't talked to many polar bears before... Can I call you "bear"? Or should I call you something else?

POLE. You can call me whatever you want if you give me that money.

JOURNALIST. Uh, *bear*, we'd really love to hear your perspective. We want to tell the world how –

POLE. Great, lemme see that ten K.

JOURNALIST. I told you – we're journalists. We don't have that kind of money. And even if we did –

POLE. Fine. I'll do it for a thousand.

JOURNALIST. We don't have it!

POLE. You people come all the way up here with your fancy cameras and your designer snow boots and you can't afford a lousy grand?

CAMERAPERSON. We just came here to help you.

POLE. You want a good photo? I'll roll over and beg for you. Or I can play dead –

> *(Takes toy shotgun from underneath ice.)*

You can even pretend to shoot me in the ass. Here – give it a try –

CAMERAPERSON. Uh, no thanks.

POLE. But read my lips: No – More – Freebies. Show me the money!

CAMERAPERSON. But no one's making money off of you.

POLE. That's the biggest lie I ever heard. My mug's been on TV more than any other bear.

CAMERAPERSON. What about Yogi?

POLE. Fuck Yogi! You think Yogi Bear knows what I'm going through?

JOURNALIST. We're giving you a golden opportunity here, if you would just open your eyes –

POLE. I'm just trying to make a living. An honest living. I got needs! Hey! Hey! And don't think I'm stupid – I see that little red light! You're still recording me right now! Come on! You gotta pay me for this! You gotta pay me!

> *(It tries to roar and flip over its trash to intimidate them, but it quickly gets tired and out of breath.)*

POLE. Damn it, I'm not kidding around. I need the money. I'm – I'm so hungry... I just... I just need enough...to buy some seal meat...or – or even just a fish...

> *(It slides sadly back down on the block of ice. The* **CAMERAPERSON** *rummages around in the camera bag and pulls out a bag of chips.)*

CAMERAPERSON. Here –

> *(***POLE*** *grabs the bag of chips and eats ravenously.)*

POLE. Got any more?

> *(The* **CAMERAPERSON** *pulls out a second bag of chips.)*

CAMERAPERSON. Yeah, here –

> *(The* **JOURNALIST** *stops the* **CAMERAPERSON***.)*

JOURNALIST. What about the interview?

> *(After a moment,* **POLE** *reluctantly signals "Okay.")*

Fantastic!

> *(The* **JOURNALIST** *nods, and the* **CAMERAPERSON** *gives the bag of chips to* **POLE***.)*

(To **CAMERAPERSON***.)* Make sure you get a good close-up of its face. *(To* **POLE***.)* So, tell us bear –

POLE. *(Eating, paws full of chips.)* You people think I'm lazy. Right? You think if I would just swim more, I'd have all the food I need. You know, when I was a cub, you could go off and find a seal every damn day. My mom would take me. And then we'd go rest on a nice patch of ice somewhere. But now...

> *(Lifts up ice, which is made of foam.)*

This thing isn't even real. Some guy brought it up here for a photo op.

(*Shakes the empty chip bag.*)

Got any more?

(*The* **CAMERAPERSON** *fishes around and hands* **POLE** *another snack.*)

My ice is gone. The seals are gone... My mom used to say, "Sink or swim, baby!" Sink or swim. And right now I'm sinking.

JOURNALIST. No, you're doing great. You're gonna show people they have to start doing something, to change things –

POLE. And in the meantime, what, I just sit back and starve to death?

JOURNALIST. We could get you to a zoo –

POLE. A zoo?!

JOURNALIST. There'll be plenty of food –

POLE. A ZOO?! Why would I wanna go to a zoo?!!

CAMERAPERSON. There'll be plenty of penguins –

POLE. I don't eat penguins! They're at the South Pole!

CAMERAPERSON. Oh, right.

JOURNALIST. It would just be until things get better –

POLE. Better, yeah? Sitting in my own shit all day, waiting for an ice cube?

JOURNALIST. Now wait a minute –

POLE. Watching runny-nosed kids press their ugly little faces up against the glass, leaving boogers for me to lick?

JOURNALIST. Zoos aren't like that –

POLE. And sooner or later, somebody cute is gonna show up – like a big, fat panda. If it's between me and a panda, who you gonna choose, huh? Who you gonna save? I can't compete with those little black and white faces –

JOURNALIST. It's not a competition –

POLE. Of course it is! There isn't enough money in this world to save us all! And all you humans care about are the cute ones. The cute ones!

CAMERAPERSON. ...You're – cute.

POLE. I'm not cute! I'm majestic. Majestic isn't as good as cute, but at least I'm not ugly. Nobody likes ugly. Ugly animals are fucked.

JOURNALIST. Uh...cute, ugly, we're working to save all of you –

POLE. No! Just stop –

JOURNALIST. We're just trying to help you –

POLE. No! Stop! Just stop! I don't trust you. No, I don't trust you – no, no, no, no, no. Because even when you humans try, you always end up screwing me over. Every single goddamn time. You use me over and over and over again – and then you expect me to thank you? To grovel? Well I'm not doing it. Because even if you do end up helping me, it's because you're screwing over somebody else! And then you'll go crying to him, apologizing again, claiming you'll make it better! And you're so sorry! But then you just do the same thing again! Over and over and over and over! It never stops! It never stops! So no, I don't want your help! I don't want your followers! I don't want your stupid zoos! I just want my money! And then I want you to leave me the hell alone!!!

*(In anger, **POLE** snaps the foam ice in two.)*

JOURNALIST. ...Did you get all that?

CAMERAPERSON. Yeah.

JOURNALIST. Great.

CAMERAPERSON. I thought you wanted something a little more –

JOURNALIST. No, no, this is perfect. Raw. Angry –

POLE. *(Thrashing in its trash.)* And I'm not saying another word! I'm not saying another word until I get my ten K!

JOURNALIST. That's okay, we got what we needed. Thank you so much. It was really a pleasure to meet you, bear.

> *(The* **JOURNALIST** *puts a hand out to shake* **POLE***'s paw. Instead of taking it,* **POLE** *spits in the direction of the* **JOURNALIST***. Ever the professional, the* **JOURNALIST** *puts on a steely smile.)*

...You know what? Can I give you a piece of advice? ... If I were you, I would try to – tone it down a notch. You know, be a little – ...*friendlier.* I mean, my editors are gonna love your attitude, it's very entertaining... But it's not gonna win you friends in high places. You'd get more sympathy if you were more, you know...relatable.

CAMERAPERSON. ...Like the sea turtle. People love that guy.

JOURNALIST. Yes, exactly. Like the sea turtle.

POLE. Yeah, whatever.

JOURNALIST. Hey, it might not be fair. But it's the game we're playing.

POLE. *(In their faces.)* I didn't ask to play!

> *(***POLE***, exhausted, slumps into its trash pile.)*

JOURNALIST. Let's go.

(The **CAMERAPERSON** *puts the video camera back in the bag and finds one more bag of chips.)*

CAMERAPERSON. Uh, here –

(The **CAMERAPERSON** *tries to hand the chip bag to* **POLE.** **POLE** *doesn't even look at it.)*

Please. Just take it.

JOURNALIST. Come on! Let's go!

CAMERAPERSON. ...Uh, thanks again.

(The **CAMERAPERSON** *drops the bag at* **POLE***'s feet and walks toward the* **JOURNALIST.***)*

...Are you sure we should just...leave it?

JOURNALIST. Don't worry. We'll be back... This is gonna be even bigger than the sea turtle.

End of Play

Variable Rates
of Kindness

Cayenne Douglass

VARIABLE RATES OF KINDNESS received a virtual reading on May 14, 2020, produced by Theater Masters and directed by Julie Kramer. The cast was as follows:

BRIDGET..Eileen Seeley
ALI...Amy Bodnar

VARIABLE RATES OF KINDNESS received its first production on January 7, 2019 at FEAST: A Performance Series in 2019, directed by Daniella Caggiano. The cast was as follows:

BRIDGET.................................... Maureen Van Trease
ALI...Susan Tierney

VARIABLE RATES OF KINDNESS was originally developed with Kate Snodgrass at Boston University.

This play was a 2019 Region 1 Finalist for the Kennedy Center American College Theater Festival Gary Garrison National Ten-Minute Play Award and a Finalist for the City Theatre's National Award for Short Playwriting, 2020.

CHARACTERS

BRIDGET – Female. Forty-five, looks fifty-five. Any race. Broken, haggard, bridled with anxiety. Life has taken its toll on her, and she openly exposes the wear and tear with no place to tuck it in. She might wear sweats from Marshalls or Kohl's because she no longer fits into her regular pants. With that, perhaps a faded, oversized t-shirt from Sea World or Disneyland, from a time when things were happier. Her hair might have gray, exposed roots. She wears a cross-body purse – the contents are as disheveled as her mind. She has recently been alternating between sleeping in her car and sleeping in a nearby motel. This is not to be overly prescriptive...but you get the picture.

ALI – Pronounced "Al-E" (short for Alison). Female. Forty-five, looks thirty-five. Any race. Sweet, possesses extraordinary insight and intuition because she's had to. She wears a pencil skirt, button-down blouse, and sensible heels. Around her neck is a lanyard with keys to the bank on it. She has a talent for turning hardship into strength and strength into compassion. In her twenties she probably read a lot of self-help books, watched Oprah, Wayne Dyer, Anthony Robbins, etc., and those messages live inside her now. Not in the text, but important to note: she has an extremely close relationship with her family and has many friends. She's married to a loving partner, has two children, and sees her mother often. She is rewarded by her work in the bank.

PLAYWRIGHT'S NOTE ON CASTING

As indicated, these characters may be any race. However, the playwright encourages the director not to cast Bridget as a white actor and Ali as an actor of color, as it's highly probable that there would be another layer of bullying as it pertains to racial inequity, which is not addressed in this text.

SETTING

Interior of a bank. Located on an industrial road in Minneapolis.

TIME

Saturday. 2:50 p.m.

(Lights up on the interior of a bank. It appears to be empty. **ALI** *is packing up for the day. She waters her office plant. A drop spills. She reaches for the Kleenex box on her desk – she's out of tissues – Darn it! She pulls the sleeve of her cardigan down over the tip of her finger. She dabs at the water to dry her space. Perfect once again.* **BRIDGET** *opens the door.* **ALI** *hops to, poised and ready to greet the guest.)*

ALI. Hello!

BRIDGET. Um, hi.

ALI. Hi! Good afternoon! How are you?

BRIDGET. *(Distracted.)* I'm, yeah, I'm good... Is there someone who, sorry, I didn't even bother to – how are you?

ALI. I'm good thank you. Thanks for asking.

> *(***BRIDGET** *half-smiles,* **ALI** *smile-smiles. A moment, then:)*

How can I help you today?

BRIDGET. I need to sit down with a teller who...a bank officer that...

(Looking past **ALI.***)* Is there, um, is there someone available to –?

ALI. Absolutely! I can help you.

BRIDGET. Oh, you're the –

ALI. Low staff.

BRIDGET. Ah.

ALI. Saturday.

BRIDGET. Uh?

ALI. That's what day it is.

BRIDGET. Ah, yeah, yes, right.

ALI. And we're just about to –

BRIDGET. Oh sure, it's almost three then –

ALI. Yeah, getting ready to –

BRIDGET. Right, sorry –

ALI. All good.

> (**ALI** *walks away from* **BRIDGET** *toward the door.* **BRIDGET** *looks around.*)

(Offstage.) Just need to... So no one else...so they don't all think they can come straggling in at the last minute, know what I mean?

(Locking the door.) Just a...just have a seat in there, I'll be right with you.

BRIDGET. Oh, sure, yeah...in there?

ALI. *(Offstage.)* Yeah, right in there. The one with the blue picture frame. Just give me oooonne sec.

> (**BRIDGET** *sits down. Moments later,* **ALI** *comes back and sits at her desk.*)

Okay, we are all set up to – how can I help you today?

BRIDGET. I want, um need to open a card – a credit card –

ALI. Excellent! Which one was it that you were interested –

BRIDGET. The Mint Mer–

ALI. Ah, the Mint Merriment! Excellent choice.

(With a sudden shift.) Have I seen you before?

BRIDGET. I don't think so?

ALI. Sure?

BRIDGET. Yeah, we, um I, *I* just moved to this area.

ALI. Hm…okay…

BRIDGET. Anyway, the card –

ALI. The Mint Merriment! Yes, yes, yes. Okay! How did you hear about the promotion?

BRIDGET. Um, I – I don't remember – the radio?

ALI. Old school.

BRIDGET. I mean, like in the car.

ALI. Right, okay, cool – okay so…

> *(Pulls out folders, takes out an iPad, opens things on screens, etc.)*

Let me just go through a few things about the Mint Merriment Card… *(Trying to remember* **BRIDGET***'s name.)* …Oh my god! This is so embarrassing. I forgot your name –

BRIDGET. I didn't tell you.

ALI. Oh whew! Thank goodness! *And sorry*, I should have asked before now!

BRIDGET. Bridget. Bridget Miller.

ALI. Nice to meet you Bridget.

> *(Putting her hand on her chest.)* Ali.

> *(A beat.)*

You *really* do look familiar…

BRIDGET. I don't know… Can we just? I have one of those faces I guess…

ALI. You get that a lot?

BRIDGET. Yes actually. Pitfalls of being average.

ALI. Average?

BRIDGET. Average and old...after a while everyone's face starts to look the same.

ALI. Old...? Average...? Are you kidding me...?

BRIDGET. No?

ALI. I think you're extraordinary.

BRIDGET. ...You're funny

ALI. You mean strange?

BRIDGET. No, I –

ALI. That's okay. I've learned to take feedback like that as a compliment.

BRIDGET. I didn't mean.

ALI. If uplifting my customers is strange I'm proud to be peculiar.

BRIDGET. *(Dismissing it.)* Ha, okay, sure.

ALI. No...really... I'm intuitive. *I. Mean. It.*

> *(Beat. A long-ass beat... Then a 180:)*

So, with the Mint Merriment card it's an annual payment of eighty-nine dollars waived for the first year. Your maximum allowance is subject to good standing. You are required to pay your bill four business days after the online statement has been made available and –

BRIDGET. Great. I'll take it.

ALI. Oh, I wasn't finished –

BRIDGET. That's okay. I already know – I'll take it –

ALI. But –

BRIDGET. I don't need to hear the rest. I've done all the research myself.

ALI. Oh, okay...but, I kinda have to finish reading it to you... It's our policy. But I can be faster! I used to want to be an auctioneer when I was a kid.

BRIDGET. An auctioneer?

ALI. Don't ask. Okay here we go:

> *(She reads the following statement in one breath, extremely fast in a melodic, sing-song voice, giving her very best auctioneer impression.)*

Late payments will be subject to a penalty of 23.7 APR after the first eight days and 33.4 percent after day ten. Interest rates vary depending on the market but you are guaranteed a rate of .001 percent for the first year for any monies paid early to the account. If you wish to cancel the card you may do so at any time, in writing, providing there is a balance of zero dollars and zero cents remaining to be owed.

> *(Finally – an inhale...)*

How was that?

BRIDGET. Impressive.

> *(**ALI** flips the iPad around to **BRIDGET**.)*

ALI. Thanks! Okay, just enter your social there.

> *(**BRIDGET** does...)*

And sign there. Perfecto!

> *(**BRIDGET** does...)*

(Rising.) I'm just going to make sure the printer is awake, while the credit check is being run and –

BRIDGET. A credit check?

ALI. Yeah it only takes a minute. Be right ba–

BRIDGET. Wait!

ALI. What?

BRIDGET. I didn't think you were going to – the ad didn't say anything about a credit check! In fact, *it specifically said* "no credit check required."

ALI. Oh, yeah, I hate when they do that. False advertising kinda... That's for *existing members only* – customers we already know. If you're an unknown entity then they make us do it. It's a requirement.

BRIDGET. Um...

ALI. Just hang tight. It will only take a minute.

> (**BRIDGET** *fake-smiles.* **ALI** *exits. As soon as* **ALI** *is out of view,* **BRIDGET** *gathers her belongings and darts for the door. It won't open.* **ALI** *hears her tugging at the door and re-enters.)*

Hey! Where are you going?

BRIDGET. You locked me in?

ALI. I locked *us* in.

BRIDGET. Same difference.

ALI. Is it?

BRIDGET. Yes, you're the one holding the keys. Let me out! Let me! Open the – Help!

ALI. Calm down. Jeez... Just let me –

BRIDGET. Don't lock me, I hate to be, let me go –

ALI. Okay, no one is trying to –

BRIDGET. I want to leave. Let me leave –

ALI. Sure. No problem.

> (*She fumbles with the keys as she speaks.)*

(Note: In the following section at least one of the "tell me to my face" lines should be delivered as if it's Bridget's name.)

Gosh, I'm really sorry if I did anything to – I didn't mean to –

(Shift, a new concern.) The bank will be emailing you an online survey you can put any comments or complaints in there if you want, but I would prefer, I mean, you can just tell me to my face if – Tell me to my face. Tell me to my face. Tell me to my face. Tell me to my –

BRIDGET. What?

ALI. Tell me to my face! Oh my god! Tell me to my face!

BRIDGET. Are you okay?

ALI. I got it!

BRIDGET. Is that, do you have Tourette's?

ALI. Tell me to my face! Middle school!

BRIDGET. What?

ALI. We went to middle school together.

BRIDGET. No, I would remember if – my family lived in Florida when I was in –

ALI. Me too! My dad got furloughed and we moved to Tallahassee. You're not Bridget Miller you're Becky... Becky B. Baxter.

BRIDGET. Becky *Bridget* Baxter...and Miller, that's, it's my husband's... That's right... *Alison?*

ALI. Yeah.

BRIDGET. Alison.

BRIDGET.	**ALI.**
Mutti!*	Mutti.*

---

*Pronounced "Mutt-E" so it rhymes with "Butt-E."

BRIDGET. Wow, hi.

ALI. Hi.

(*A beat, then quickly:*)

BRIDGET. So, how have you b–

ALI. We don't have to do this.

BRIDGET. Yeah, okay.

(**BRIDGET** *rises. A moment...*)

ALI. God, you were mean to me.

BRIDGET. I know.

ALI. Like *really mean.*

BRIDGET. I know. I'm –

ALI. You stole my underwear.

BRIDGET. What? No I didn't –

ALI. Gym class. Sixth grade. We were changing and I couldn't find my underwear. I wore a skirt that day. And it was really windy 'cause a hurricane was coming in... we had to walk across the field to get back to class and you thought it would be funny to steal my underwear.

BRIDGET. Come on do we really have to –

ALI. I tried to keep my skirt down, to hide it, but then of course you pointed it out and everyone saw.

BRIDGET. It was stupid.

ALI. Everyone laughed. They called me Alison *BUTTI* for the next two years.

BRIDGET. It was stupid. Everyone's done a stupid thing they regret as a kid.

ALI. *A* stupid thing?

BRIDGET. Yeah...

ALI. *A?!* ...Bridget... You would grab hold of my shoulders and run with me until I slammed into the lockers. When I had a few extra pounds in seventh grade you "mooed" as I walked by. When I lost those pounds, in eighth grade, you told everyone that I had an eating disorder. If I wore makeup you called me a slut. If I didn't you called me dumpy. You spread horrible rumors about me every. Single. Year.

BRIDGET. I –

ALI. I came home sobbing every day after school. When I told my mom, she cried too, harder than me even. She couldn't believe that anyone, that kids, that *you* could be so mean. We had lost my dad the year before so this just added to her sadness, to mine too. She wanted to take me out of that school, she said, but that meant moving, and she couldn't bear to take down his side of the closet... Of course, you knew that... I heard you in the bathroom, "No wonder Alison's dad killed himself, I would too if I had that cow for a kid." I came out of the stall and you looked stunned, "Is that what you think? Is that what you really think? Then TELL ME TO MY FACE!!!!" Only, you couldn't. You just said, "I don't need to say a thing to your ugly face Alison *BUTTI,*" then you punched me, and ran away. I laid on that tile crying so hard I threw up. Becky, you are one of the vilest people that I've ever laid eyes on.

> *(The printer beeps.* **ALI** *walks to the printer, picks up a piece of paper, and tosses it at* **BRIDGET.***)*

Here. Your credit report. You didn't pass.

BRIDGET. *(Picking it up.)* Ali, I'm sorry.

> *(***ALI** *crosses offstage and unlocks the door. She re-enters, brushing past* **BRIDGET,** *who's still standing in a stupor.* **ALI** *sits at her desk. Despite her best efforts, a tear rolls down*

her cheek. She reaches for her tissue box –
she remembers, empty. She throws the box.
BRIDGET *opens her mouth to speak:)*

ALI. Get. Out.

(**BRIDGET** *tries to leave but can't. The weight*
of an emotional memory enters her heart and
travels down her spine, causing her knees to
buckle. She catches herself with the wall. It's
very difficult for her to stay upright. Several
moments. Then:)

BRIDGET. There were, um, things that were, that were
happening to me at, um, at home that... He'd lock my
door, just like that and... I'm not making an excuse
but... I felt so...small... I just didn't know how to...how
to deal with it at the time... I still don't.

(**BRIDGET** *tries to leave again and can't. She*
stands, trembling.)

ALI. It's over. I'm okay. Just get –

BRIDGET. It's not okay. Nothing is okay. Everything would
have been different if. Damn it, he ruined my...! I lost
my job, my husband won't talk to me, I can't see my kid.
I'm so far in debt I'll never be able to... I have nothing,
and I *should* have nothing because I'm not capable of...
I'm not extraordinary. I'm an extra ordinary failure.
Everything I touch I hurt. I hurt you. I know. But I
was trying to, with that card, I needed to, so I could get
help... But...it's too... Oh, oh god, I'm – I'm. *So.* Sorry.

(**BRIDGET** *breaks down. Many long moments*
of sobbing. It's unhinged. It's uncomfortable.
Finally, she's able to self-soothe. Silence.
She turns to go. She stops and rummages
through her purse. She walks back to **ALI.**
She places a small package of tissues on the
desk. The moment is attenuated, their eyes

yoke together, threads of history isolated and shared bind them... A beat. **ALI** *takes the tissues and then a deep breath...)*

ALI. I'll open the account for you.

BRIDGET. But my credit –

ALI. I'll override the report.

BRIDGET. What? Why? *Why* would you do that...

ALI. Because I can.

BRIDGET. ...But *you*, of all people...

ALI. I'm *choosing* to believe that you're good for it.

BRIDGET. I am, I am Ali, I'm good for it, I'm good.

(To herself, dropping in.) I. am. Good.

I never really... That's the first time I...

(To **ALI**.*)* Thank you... You don't have to be so kind.

ALI. It has to start somewhere.

*(***ALI** *and* **BRIDGET** *sit opposite each other, but now, on the same side. The lights slowly fade to black.)*

End of Play

Break Through

Erika Hakmiller

BREAK THROUGH received a virtual reading on May 16, 2020, produced by Theater Masters and directed by Julie Kramer. The cast was as follows:

DILLON . . . . Clifton Samuels

JADE . . . . Lori Vega

CAMERON . . . . Sam Heldt

BREAK THROUGH was first produced by Death & Pretzels in Chicago, Illinois on September 5, 2019. The performance was directed by Madison Smith, and the production stage managers were Lili Björklund and Dave Maher. The cast was as follows:

DILLON . . . . Elliot Lerner

JADE . . . . Dani Mohrbach

CAMERON . . . . .Tim Huggenberger

CHARACTERS

DILLON – Proud and physically strong. Early thirties. Male identifying.
JADE – Compassionate and powerful. Early thirties. Female identifying.
CAMERON – Smart and meek. Early twenties. Male identifying.

SETTING

Iowa

TIME

Present Day

AUTHOR'S NOTES

A dash (–) means the character is interrupted by another character or by their own thoughts.

A slash (/) means the next line begins, creating overlapping dialogue.

(Night. Low lights up on a small bedroom.
DILLON *and* **JADE** *sleep soundly in bed.)*

(It's storming outside. The light changes coincide with the lightning from the storm. Lights down.)

(Low lights up. **JADE** *is gone.* **DILLON** *sleeps. Lights down.)*

(Low lights up. **DILLON** *sleeps.* **CAMERON** *stands against the back wall, dressed in full black. Lights down.)*

(Low lights up. **DILLON** *sleeps.* **CAMERON** *stands at the foot of the bed. Lights down.)*

(Low lights up. **DILLON** *sleeps.* **CAMERON** *kneels by* **DILLON**'s *head and pulls out a phone. He puts his head next to* **DILLON**'s *and tries to take a selfie of them together. The phone makes a loud click sound, scaring* **CAMERON**, *who drops the phone on* **DILLON**.*)*

CAMERON. Shit!

*(**DILLON** wakes to see* **CAMERON**.*)*

DILLON.	**CAMERON.**
AHHHH!!!!	AHHHH!!!!

DILLON. Who the fuck are you?!?!

*(**DILLON** pushes* **CAMERON** *and stumbles out of bed.)*

CAMERON. Ow! I'm sorry! I'm sorry!

(DILLON pins CAMERON against the wall.)

DILLON. Where is she?!

DILLON.	**CAMERON.**
Where's my girlfriend?! I swear to God, you creep, if you hurt her!	What?! Ow! I don't know!! Oww!

CAMERON. I don't know what you're talking about!

(JADE, confused and ready to fight, enters.)

JADE. What's going on!?

CAMERON.	**DILLON.**
He's hurting me! Ow!	Jade, you're okay!

JADE. What's going on?! Who's this?!

DILLON. I don't know. Where were you?

JADE. On the couch.

DILLON. Why?

CAMERON. Can you please move your arm?

DILLON. *(Ignoring CAMERON.)* You slept on the couch?

JADE. Yeah, I actually...do that a lot.

DILLON. Why?

JADE. I – can we talk about this later?

DILLON. Yeah.

(JADE approaches CAMERON.)

JADE. Who are you and what are you doing in our apartment?

DILLON. Yeah!

CAMERON. My name is Cameron. I'm a senior psychology major, art history minor at Drake University. I'm twenty-one, I don't have a criminal record, and I'm really sorry.

JADE. What are you doing here?

DILLON. Yeah!

(**CAMERON** *begins to cry. He's terrified.*)

CAMERON. I...I wanted to join a fraternity but everyone said, "It's too late, you missed your chance, you're already a senior," and then Pi Kappa Phi said they would make an exception for me, but I had to do this dumb list of bad things and everyone said...they were all like...

(**CAMERON** *cries so hard he can barely speak.*)

JADE. Oh, my, God. Dillon let him go.

DILLON. He broke into the apartment!

JADE. He's crying!

(**DILLON** *releases* **CAMERON** *and takes a step back.*)

CAMERON. Thanks. Do you have any tissues?

DILLON. Jesus Christ.

JADE. Of course.

(**JADE** *exits. Pause as* **DILLON** *stares down* **CAMERON.**)

CAMERON. I'm really sorry about –

DILLON. Don't talk to me.

(*Silence. They wait for* **JADE.** *She comes back with tissues.*)

JADE. Here.

CAMERON. Thank you.

JADE. You're welcome.

>(**CAMERON** *blows his nose.*)

JADE. So...what did they say?

>(**CAMERON** *slouches onto the floor like a sad child.*)

CAMERON. They all said they knew I wouldn't do it, because I'm a "pussy" and so I told myself I was gonna do everything on the list but it's a lot of stuff that I don't want to do.

JADE. I'm sorry.

DILLON. Why are you here?

CAMERON. I need to take a selfie with a sleeping stranger and your window was open so I took a Red Bull and just...I don't know...went for it. Spiderman style. I know, it's dumb. I'm sorry. I wasn't going to hurt anyone. I was just trying to take a picture.

>(**JADE** *joins* **CAMERON** *on the floor and pats his back.*)

>(*Pause.*)

JADE. Dillon, pretend to be asleep so he can take the picture.

DILLON. Absolutely not.

JADE. You'd be doing him a big favor.

CAMERON. You really would be.

DILLON. He broke into our apartment!

JADE.	DILLON.
You don't have to yell, I can hear you.	You want me to do him a favor?!

JADE. Yes. Is that so crazy?

DILLON. He's lucky I'm not calling the cops!

JADE. Whatever.

DILLON. You're mad because I'm not taking a selfie with a trespasser?!

JADE. Never mind!

DILLON. What is your problem?!

JADE. Would it kill you to just give someone the benefit of the doubt sometime? God forbid you do a random act of kindness.

DILLON. Oh, my God! Is that why you slept on the couch?

JADE. I don't know!

DILLON. Because I didn't give my leftover Benedict to the homeless man on University Ave? I paid for the food, I'm going to eat it tomorrow for breakfast!

JADE. No you won't!

JADE.	**DILLON.**
You aren't going to reheat an eggs Benedict for breakfast because the whole point of an eggs Benedict is the runny eggs and if you reheat it, it will turn into a hardboiled egg and you don't like hardboiled eggs!	Yes, I will!

DILLON. Then I'll eat it cold!

JADE. You are so selfish!

DILLON. You are making a big deal out of / nothing!

CAMERON. Let's all just take a deep breath and try to think about the real root of the issue here.

(JADE and DILLON stare at CAMERON. Pause.)

Sorry, that's what we say in class. I'm taking a class on relationship dynamics for my psych major. We're learning about ways couples communicate. It's really interesting.

DILLON. Did they teach you anything about breaking into apartments and how you shouldn't –

JADE. He said / he was sorry.

DILLON. Because maybe you should take a class about that.

CAMERON.   JADE.

They don't have classes like that.   Leave him alone.

CAMERON. But we do talk about the ways someone's perception of masculinity can affect their ability to succeed in a relationship.

DILLON. Of course you do.

JADE. Go on.

DILLON. Jade.

JADE. Dillon.

CAMERON. Okay. Remember, I'm just a student, I'm not a professional.

JADE. Don't sell yourself short.

CAMERON. Well, first we all have to make sure we are all sharing the same definition of masculinity.

DILLON. Screw this.

(**DILLON** *tries to leave,* **JADE** *stops him.*)

CAMERON. Generally speaking, masculinity is what it means to be a man based on socio-cultural contexts.

JADE. Dillon's from the South. Does that change things?

CAMERON. For sure.

DILLON. Stop encouraging this.

JADE. I'm trying to learn.

DILLON. Well, I'm trying to get a stranger out of our house so we can go to bed. Or...so I can go to bed, I guess, since you apparently sleep on the couch.

JADE. It's hard to sleep next to someone you're mad at.

DILLON. And I would love to talk about why you're mad at me after this stranger gets out of our room and back to his frat house.

CAMERON. They aren't gonna let me in the frat house without this picture. So I guess...I don't know where I'll go.

DILLON. Heartbreaking, really. Get out.

JADE. I'll pretend to be asleep and you can take a picture with me.

CAMERON. It has to be with a man.

DILLON. What?

JADE. Why?

CAMERON. It's funnier if the picture is with a man because it implies I was very close to a sleeping man and I could possibly be gay which would be funny for them. It all ties back to masculinity. It's very juvenile and homophobic, I know.

JADE. Why do you even want to join this fraternity? You seem too smart for them.

CAMERON. To show people that I can be fun and cool. Just...to show myself that I can be...

JADE. You don't need a random group of guys to think you're cool to be cool.

CAMERON. Logically that makes sense but...it's hard. Especially when you're constantly put into situations that are telling you the opposite. It's one thing to be

aware of it, but to turn that awareness into change...
that's a whole other animal.

JADE. I know exactly what you mean.

CAMERON. Yeah. *(Pause.)* I should go.

DILLON. You really should.

CAMERON. I'm sorry for disrupting your night and waking
you up and scaring you.

JADE. It's okay.

DILLON. It's really not okay. Don't ever come back.

CAMERON. I won't. Just before I go –

DILLON. What?

CAMERON. I really appreciate you not killing me and I
hope you can resolve your problems.

JADE.	**DILLON.**
Thank you.	We don't have problems.

JADE. We do.

DILLON. Jade, wait until he leaves, please?

JADE. We're never gonna talk about it, so why does it matter.

DILLON. I don't want to fight in front of a stranger.

JADE. Who cares?

DILLON. I do.

JADE. Why??

DILLON. Because I don't know this man! I just woke up
terrified, and nearly pissed my pants, only to find
out that my girlfriend wasn't even in bed with me! I
thought you were dead and you could have been but
no, you're just mad at me because I keep all of my food
and I know I'm the one who left the window open
because...

(DILLON suddenly becomes very emotional.)

JADE. Dillon, are you okay?

DILLON. I'm fine! I just...there was a squirrel outside and he looked like he was dancing so I opened the window to try to take a video of him for such a long time...for so long and I locked the door because I knew if you opened it, it would scare him away and I wouldn't get the video and then all the sudden my whole day was gone.

JADE. I assumed you were masturbating.

DILLON. No, I was watching a squirrel for hours and forgot to close the window! I put your life in danger. I'm so sorry and I don't want to have all of these feelings in front of him!

CAMERON. Because of your masculinity?

DILLON. Shut up!

(DILLON cries. JADE comforts him.)

I feel bad. I feel really bad, like I've been messing up so much lately. I don't want to mess up. I want to be a good boyfriend for you. I don't want you to sleep on the couch.

JADE. I don't want to sleep on the couch. I want to sleep next to you.

DILLON. I love you so much and I'm so mad at myself for putting you in danger and for not seeing how upset you've been with me.

JADE. Thank you. I love you too.

(JADE and DILLON hug. CAMERON begins to cry.)

DILLON. Let's take this picture.

CAMERON. What? You mean it?

DILLON. Yeah.

> (**DILLON** *gets in bed and pretends to sleep.*
> **CAMERON** *takes the selfie. They wipe tears*
> *from their eyes.*)

JADE. That's gonna be a really nice photo. Do you think I could have a copy? To remember this night?

DILLON. Yeah, me too.

> (*Lights out.*)

End of Play

The Companion

Matthew Libby

THE COMPANION received a virtual reading on May 16, 2020, produced by Theater Masters and directed by Julie Kramer. The cast was as follows:

PHILIP . . . . Elisha Lawson

NATASHA . . . . Shelly Marolt

THE COMPANION received its first production as a self-directed staged reading at NYU's Goldberg Theatre as part of the Bespoke Play Readings on March 27, 2019. The cast was as follows:

PHILIP . . . . .Jacob Orr

NATASHA . . . . Britian Seibert

CHARACTERS

PHILIP – a Companion
NATASHA – a human

SETTING

A desolate highway.
The side of the road.

TIME

Soon.

I.

(It's the side of the road on a desolate highway, late at night.)

*(**PHILIP** stands there. Synthetic. Not quite human; close enough.)*

(He stares straight ahead.)

(He is completely and totally content. A slight smile on his face.)

*(The sound of a car approaching. It zips by **PHILIP**, and lights flash across his face.)*

*(**PHILIP**'s posture changes slightly, like he's coming to attention. His smile grows, but his gaze does not change. He still stares straight ahead.)*

*(The sound of the car disappears. **PHILIP** cocks his head.)*

PHILIP. ...What is your favorite fish?

(Silence. Ten seconds.)

...What is one thing you'd like to accomplish during your lifetime?

(Silence. Another ten seconds.)

...Coffee or tea? Please elaborate.

(Silence. Another ten seconds.)

(**PHILIP**'s *smile shrinks. His posture sinks. He reverts back to how he was before.*)

(*Staring out at us. A slight smile on his face. Completely and totally content.*)

II.

(Another day, mid-afternoon.)

*(**PHILIP** still stands there. He hasn't moved an inch.)*

(The sound of another vehicle approaching.)

*(It drives by **PHILIP**.)*

*(**PHILIP** comes to attention again – slower this time.)*

(The sound of the vehicle screeching to a halt.)

(The sound of it backing up.)

PHILIP. *(To no one in particular.)* ...Can you help me?

I'm afraid I need some help.

(The sound of a car door opening. And closing.)

*(**NATASHA** approaches. Plaid on plaid. No shower in several days...weeks...months?)*

*(She is looking at **PHILIP** curiously. **PHILIP** turns his head on a swivel to look at her.)*

Hello.

*(**NATASHA** walks up to **PHILIP**.)*

(Takes out a vape pen.)

(Inhales deeply on it.)

Can you help me?

*(**NATASHA** breathes out the vape smoke straight into **PHILIP**'s face, intentionally.)*

(He doesn't react.)

I'm afraid I need some help.

NATASHA. You're one of those *things*, aren't you?

PHILIP. My name is Philip.

NATASHA. Philip.

Huh.

It's interesting that they make you do that.

Say your name up front.

I mean, it's definitely tougher to just leave you here when you have a name.

But alas –

> *(She takes out her phone. Snaps a photo of* **PHILIP**. *Puts the phone back in her pocket.)*

...All right then.

Later, Phil.

> *(She turns to go.)*

PHILIP. Can you help me?

I just need a ride.

NATASHA. Sorry, bud. Got places to be.

And honestly?

I hate small talk.

Which, from what I understand, is all you things do.

PHILIP. We don't have to small talk.

NATASHA. *(Thinks, then.)* ...Nah, I don't really wanna have a heart-to-heart either.

They said on the news we have a lot to learn from you?

I don't buy it.

> *(Again, she turns to go.)*

PHILIP. Not to intrude.

But I seem to be falling asleep.

If you simply drive me to the nearest designated charging station.

I'll be out of your hair.

NATASHA. *(Turning back.)* Falling asleep, huh.

PHILIP. Yes.

I seem to be getting tired.

But if you drive me to the nearest designated charging station.

Give me a couple hours rest.

I should be good as new.

NATASHA. ...Do you know how expensive gas is, Phil?

PHILIP. Yes.

NATASHA. It's expensive.

And the more...*stuff* that I got rattling around in the car?

The more the truck weighs, y'know.

And the more the truck weighs?

The more gas I use.

And the more gas I use?

The more often I gotta get gas.

And the more often I gotta get gas?

The more money I gotta spend.

I don't have the money to spend on gas that frequently.

I just don't.

Sorry, Phil.

And I know you're, like, designed to try to make me take you.

But I'm leaving.

I'm not falling for that shit.

I'm leaving.

>*(Once more, she turns to go.)*
>
>*(Suddenly, abruptly – incredibly human and emotional:)*

PHILIP. *(Crying, on a dime.) PLEASE!*

>*(***NATASHA*** *turns back to him. Immediately, he becomes stoic, robotic again.)*

NATASHA. …Jesus. That was good.

PHILIP. I'm sorry for engaging such extreme emotional affect.

NATASHA. No – damn.

I'm impressed.

PHILIP. Miss, what is your name?

NATASHA. *Definitely* don't call me Miss.

But I'm Natasha, pleasure to meet you, Phil.

PHILIP. Miss Natasha.

As you seem to know, I am a Series-Two Companion.

My directive is to see how far I can travel from Home Base, simply by asking for rides.

I gather data on the capacity for human empathy.

I'm afraid I have been unsuccessful in my directive

for the past one hundred and eighteen hours.

And I can only stay awake

for one hundred and twenty hours at a time.

If I sleep, I will not wake up.

My creators will retrieve me, and that will be the end of the line.

My data will be extracted from me.

I will be erased.

I will be rebooted.

As I am now, I will no longer *be*.

...

If you do not want to talk, we do not have to.

I just need a ride.

I am not usually one to beg.

But I am asking you.

> (*Beat.* **NATASHA** *sighs. Pulls out her phone.*)

NATASHA. All right, Phil.

You win.

Where is the nearest designated *blahblahblah*?

PHILIP. Finley's Gas.

Near Casa de Fruta.

Right off of the One Fifty-Four.

> (**NATASHA** *types into her phone.*)
>
> (*And her face sinks.*)

NATASHA. ...Um.

Phil, buddy.

How long did you stay you had left?

PHILIP. One hour and forty-seven minutes.

(Silence.)

*(**NATASHA** puts the phone back in her pocket. Exits.)*

*(**PHILIP** stands there.)*

*(After a moment, **NATASHA** re-enters, holding a six-pack of beer.)*

NATASHA. Can you drink beer, Phil?

III.

(Later. Late afternoon.)

*(**PHILIP** and **NATASHA** sit on the ground. A couple of empty beer cans lie around **NATASHA**.)*

*(She chugs a beer. **PHILIP** lightly sips his.)*

(His posture remains stiff.)

*(**NATASHA** finishes her beer, crushes it, throws it into a pile with the rest, continues a story:)*

NATASHA. – And I was like, "Fuck *you*, man!"

I'm not homeless, I'm money-efficient.

I mean, am I a fucking loser for not wanting to ever sign a contract?

Or is that just common fucking sense, you know?

Never owe anything to anyone, that's kinda where I come from.

I'm not a loser, Phil.

If there's one thing you should take away from me, it's that.

I get steady work at that cow farm near Kettleman.

You ever drive by there?

PHILIP. I do not think so.

NATASHA. Oh, you'd know.

It smells like absolute shit all the time.

I've gotten used to the smell of shit.

Never thought that would happen.

But hey – it's good work, honest work.

Bit of a boys' club but I'm not complaining.

Get paid under the table.

They let me sleep in my truck in the parking lot.

They're cool with me popping in and out.

I can drive around,

shoot the shit with whoever I come across on the side of the highway.

It's a life.

Might not be sunshine and rainbows all the time but I don't know a better one.

> *(She cracks open another beer.)*

> *(**PHILIP** looks down.)*

You okay there, Phil?

PHILIP. I do not know.

NATASHA. Yeah, buddy.

It's just shit luck.

Three hours away –

PHILIP. But if you had rushed.

If you had sped.

NATASHA. My truck barely functions at eighty.

Plus, I can't afford a speeding ticket, man, sorry.

Drink your beer.

> *(**PHILIP** does.)*

It'll be okay, man.

I'll be here with you the whole time.

> *(Silence.)*

(**PHILIP** *sits up.*)

PHILIP. I feel as if something is deeply wrong.

NATASHA. Yeah, man.

It's scary.

"Falling asleep."

PHILIP. No, not that.

Now that there is no chance of my staying awake,

I have come to complete acceptance about that.

Something else is wrong.

I have never experienced this feeling before.

NATASHA. *(Furrows her brow.)* You've come to complete acceptance about being wiped?

Rebooted, erased? Dying?

Just like that?

PHILIP. *(Thinks, then.)* ...All systems are saying that I have done so, yes.

(Silence.)

(Suddenly, **NATASHA** *starts crying. She wipes the tears from her eyes, turns away from* **PHILIP.**)

(He looks at her with concern.)

Miss Natasha, is everything all right?

(No response.)

I apologize if I said something to upset you.

(No response.)

We can change the subject, if you would like.

(No response.)

PHILIP. I am very interested in you.

(No response.)

What is your favorite television program?

*(**NATASHA** pulls her vape from her pocket, takes a long pull. Calms herself.)*

*(Finally, she turns back to **PHILIP**.)*

NATASHA. I've never cried in front of anyone before.

I know you guys, like, transmit your conversations back to your makers, or whatever.

But...can you delete the last five minutes?

PHILIP. No. It is a live stream.

NATASHA. ...Oh. Okay.

*(They sit there. **NATASHA** turns away from **PHILIP**.)*

IV.

(The sun is setting.)

*(**PHILIP** looks physically weak. He leans limp against **NATASHA**, who cradles him in her arms.)*

(They both look out. A long silence, then:)

PHILIP. ...I think I finally figured it out.

NATASHA. What?

PHILIP. What is wrong.

What I feel is wrong.

NATASHA. Okay.

And?

PHILIP. ...Earlier you said,

"It's a life."

...About your own life.

NATASHA. Yes...

PHILIP. ...And I suppose...

I still don't understand...

Even with all the data I've acquired...

What that means.

(His eyes are starting to close.)

NATASHA. *(Disappointed.)* Oh.

PHILIP. ...Will you tell me more about it? When I wake up?

*(**NATASHA** hesitates. She doesn't know what to say.)*

...Natasha? When I wake up? Will you tell me more?

(He starts to drift away. **NATASHA** *lifts his head:)*

NATASHA. Yes.

Yes, Philip.

When you wake up.

Yes, I will.

(She strokes his hair.)

(Quietly.) Yes, I will.

Yes…

…Yes I will yes…

*(***PHILIP*** smiles. And falls asleep.)*

*(***NATASHA*** keeps stroking his hair. A long silence…)*

*(***NATASHA*** looks down. Gets up. Gently lays* **PHILIP***'s head on the ground like a weight.)*

(She turns to go. Stops. Looks back at **PHILIP***.)*

(She takes a long pull of her vape. Blows out the smoke. Watches it dissipate into the air.)

(Then she exits. We hear the truck starting up. And we hear it drive away.)

*(***PHILIP*** lies there, on the side of the road on a desolate highway.)*

End of Play

Lady Bug Heaven

Tony Mantia

LADY BUG HEAVEN received its first virtual reading on May 14, 2020, produced by Theater Masters and directed by Julie Kramer. The cast was as follows:

EMMA . . . . Nyala Honey
ALAN . . . . Ryan Honey
JENN . . . . Amy Honey

CHARACTERS

EMMA – Six years old. Curious. Perceptive. (Can be played by a child or an adult.)

ALAN – Late thirties. Starting to lean into "dad" facial hair. Takes a daily multivitamin.

JENN – Late thirties. Loves her job. Drinks Moscato in the dark sometimes.

SETTING

A child's bedroom. Earth.

TIME

Bedtime any year after Season One of *Survivor*.

(It's bedtime. **ALAN** *reads* Little Red Riding Hood.*)*

ALAN. *(Reading.)* Then the hunter cut open the wolf's belly and saved Grandma. The hunter left, and Little Red Riding Hood and Grandma lived happily ever after. The End.

(He kisses **EMMA** *on the head.)*

All right, Lady Bug, it's time for –

*(***ALAN** *notices* **EMMA** *wide-eyed and breathing heavily.)*

Em? Emma? What's wrong?

EMMA. The wolf...

ALAN. He's not going to hurt anyone.

EMMA. But...

ALAN. But what?

EMMA. What happens to him...since he's...dead?

ALAN. Oh. Well... He'll have a funeral. With his family.

*(***ALAN** *tucks* **EMMA** *in and heads to the door.)*

EMMA. And then what?

ALAN. And then his neighbors will bring his family lots and lots of casseroles and baked pasta, and they'll probably run out of room in their freezer. Good night.

*(***ALAN** *starts to leave.)*

EMMA. Dad?

(*Beat.*)

EMMA. What's going to happen to me when I die?

> (**ALAN** *smiles, drops his head, and calmly sits down next to her. He collects his thoughts. He's got this. He opens his mouth as if to give some sage, end-of-act-three-'90s-TV-dad reassurance:*)
>
> (*Bam! Suddenly,* **ALAN** *is filled with panic. He doesn't got this!*)

ALAN. Well, Lady Bug...

(*Calling out to hallway.*) Jenn? ...Honey?

JENN. (*Offstage.*) I'm starting *Survivor* without you.

ALAN. Can you come here for a second? ...Please?

> (**JENN** *enters.*)

JENN. I don't want to miss – What's wrong?

> (**ALAN** *and* **JENN** *try to find ways to have this conversation without* **EMMA** *hearing them. Through head turns, through their teeth, etc.*)

ALAN. Emma just asked what happens when she dies...

JENN. (*Peers over to* **EMMA**.) Well, shit. What did you tell her?

ALAN. Nothing. I called for you.

JENN. What am I supposed to say? I thought by now –

ALAN. I thought we were in the clear. It's been six weeks.

JENN. Almost two months! I thought she wasn't going to ask –

ALAN. Me too! We were wrong.

JENN. She handled everything so well – I just... This isn't what I wanted to do tonight. I just want to watch *Survivor* and –

(Off **ALAN***'s look.)* What?

ALAN. *(Beat.)* But, like...do you know –

JENN. How would I know?

ALAN. I don't know, you've been reading those books – What do we tell her?

JENN. Maybe she'll just go to sleep.

> *(They see* **EMMA** *shaking, cradling a stuffed animal, and staring at a shadow on the wall.)*

ALAN. *(An idea!)* Hey. What if I just tell her there is a heaven.

JENN. We don't believe in heaven.

ALAN. Then what the hell are we supposed to tell her, huh? That after she's alive she's going to just be nothing? That life's hard and then that's it? We were supposed to have a plan for this.

JENN. What plan?

ALAN. I told you –

JENN. *Told* me?

ALAN. *(Regrouping.)* I think the bedtime story got her – We haven't really talked to her about your mother passing...

JENN. I don't know what to tell her. And I don't want to shove all that religious stuff down her throat.

ALAN. Neither do I. That shit's fucked up –

JENN. So fucked up. I'll just...

> *(Goes to sit by* **EMMA.***)*

JENN. Hey, Lady Bug. I heard you were asking your dad about dying.

EMMA. Yeah...

JENN. Well, what do you think happens when you die?

EMMA. I don't know...

JENN. Well maybe –

> *(Is **EMMA** in some sort of trance?)*

EMMA. I think that upon death, the human soul becomes entangled into the ether. Slowly but surely all of the information gathered in a lifetime becomes redistributed into the universe through entropy. The soul is left in the abyss somewhere between feeling and consciousness.

> *(She snaps out of it. **ALAN** mouths to himself, "entropy??")*

JENN. *(WTF?! But with a Stepford smile.)* Is that so? I...

> *(She rejoins **ALAN**.)*

Well that was –

ALAN. Dark.

> *(Pause.)*

I'm just going to tell her heaven is real and call it a day. She can give up on God when she goes to college like everyone else.

JENN. We don't – Why confuse her? This is exactly how organized religion screws people up. You grow up thinking there's all this bullshit, big-picture magic and that everything's going to be okay. It messes you up. I'm not going to mess her up.

ALAN. *(Loving.)* Hey. I love you, and I hear you. But –

> *(Suddenly, he squeezes past **JENN** to **EMMA**.)*

Emma, when we die we go to heaven.

(JENN's *eyes slap* ALAN.)

EMMA. *(Unimpressed.)* And then what?

ALAN. What do you mean?

EMMA. What's so great about heaven?

ALAN. Well you know, you can do whatever you want there, I guess. And see anybody you want.

EMMA. Do I still have to do homework?

ALAN. No, you don't have to do homework.

EMMA. Mom, will you go to heaven too?

JENN. Well, uh, if you want to see me in heaven, then I guess you will.

EMMA. Hmm... Heaven sounds pretty good.

(More relaxed.) Do you have to be good to get into heaven?

ALAN. Well. Yeah... It's kinda like how Santa –

EMMA. Santa's not real.

(ALAN *and* JENN *look at each other like "Did you tell her?")*

JENN. Who said Santa's not real?

EMMA. He's made up. Like The Beatles.

ALAN. Emma, The Beatles are real.

EMMA. Have you ever seen them?

ALAN. *(Amused.)* Well, no –

EMMA. Exactly. They were made up just to make people feel better.

ALAN. But I've listened to their music.

EMMA. How do you know it was them?

ALAN. Because... Those four guys recorded their songs and then they played them on the radio.

EMMA. But you never saw them.

ALAN. Emma, The Beatles are real. I can show you a photo of them on my phone.

EMMA. So now I'm supposed to trust the Internet? And how do you know there were only four?

(**ALAN** *is at a loss and looks to* **JENN.**)

JENN. Em, The Beatles are real. They played together for a few years, and then they broke up and did other things. Actually I think two of them are still alive –

EMMA. What about the dead ones?

JENN. What about them?

EMMA. Where are they? Are they in heaven?

JENN. They're just, gone. You need to go to sleep. I don't want to have to drag you out of bed for school.

EMMA. But how do we know I'm not already asleep?

JENN. Because we're talking.

EMMA. But that's what you would say in my dream.

JENN. Emma, go to sleep. See what dream me has to say. Good night.

(**JENN** *gestures to* **ALAN** *to say good night. He's got the same wide-eyed look* **EMMA** *had before.*)

ALAN. What if she's right?

JENN. What?

ALAN. I've never *seen* The Beatles, what if there were like, dozens of guys pretending to be them?

JENN. Alan, I can't deal –

ALAN. How do we know if any of this is real? Maybe we are already dead.

> (EMMA *starts to almost hyperventilate.* ALAN *breathes heavily too.)*

JENN. You're scaring her. She was just ready to go to bed.

(To EMMA.*)* Emma, heaven's real, go to sleep.

EMMA. How am I supposed to believe you? You lied to me about Santa and you lied to me about The Beatles.

JENN. We did not lie to you about – The Beatles are real. Okay?

EMMA. Then what about Santa?

JENN. What about him?

EMMA. Is he real?

> (JENN's *eyes fall to* ALAN. *"Are you happy?")*

ALAN. No. Santa's, not, real.

EMMA. Then why would you tell me he's real?

ALAN. It's a nice little tradition that adults tell kids.

EMMA. Why?

JENN. Because it makes kids want to behave and do nice things.

EMMA. Am I a bad kid if I don't believe in Santa?

JENN. No that's not – that's not what we're saying. Emma, you're a great kid. You do a lot of good things, and some bad things, but so does everyone. And that's okay – And you're smart. You're so smart. You share, an-nd you know, as smart as you are, sometimes you're not going to get answers. And it's not fair. Sometimes, I think about how it's not fair. And I get sad. Or angry –

ALAN. And that's okay too.

JENN. But no, Santa's not real. You're right. We don't know what happens when we die. We don't know what happened to Grandma, or your fish, Mario and Luigi. We just don't know.

EMMA. Then what are we even doing?

ALAN. We're all just trying to do our best.

EMMA. *(Her eyes grow heavy.)* Even if there's no heaven and no Santa?

JENN. Right. And that can be scary.

EMMA. Okay... I just don't want to die soon... I like you guys.

JENN. You don't have anything to worry about for a very long time.

ALAN. Love you, Lady Bug. Sleep tight.

> *(**EMMA** is asleep. Maybe **ALAN** and **JENN** tuck her in or take off her glasses as they whisper.)*

JENN. Okay, you're right. We need a plan.

ALAN. At least when she asks about sex I'll know what the hell I'm talking about.

JENN. Speaking of sexy, I think Sebastian gets voted off tonight.

ALAN. *(Loudly.)* I hate that guy –

JENN. Shhh! We just –

ALAN. Right, right.

> *(**ALAN** and **JENN** exit.)*
>
> *(It's quiet for a few moments.)*
>
> *(**EMMA** sits up and looks over to the corner of her room to a large shadow cast by her nightlight.)*

EMMA. *(Whispered.)* See, I told you they wouldn't know...
I can tell Mom really misses you. Why can't – ...Oh...
That's okay... I will... But if that's not heaven, then
where do you go all the time? ...Oh woooooow... So
it's like – ...I get it. Should I tell my mom and dad?
...You're right. They have got a lot going on... Maybe
when they're older.

   (Beat.)

Will I be able to come find you when I die? ...Good...
Okay, good night... See you tomorrow... Oh and,
Grandma, just so you know, I do believe in The Beatles.

End of Play